KRAKUS, KRAKUS...

or

THE INCREDIBLE
ADVENTURE
OF
MR. SKOLA'S
TOURIST CLUB

by Mirko Gabler

Henry Holt and Company · New York

For Mr. Skola   —M. G.

First edition
Published by Henry Holt and Company, Inc.,
115 West 18th Street, New York, New York 10011.
Published simultaneously in Canada by Fitzhenry & Whiteside Ltd.,
91 Granton Drive, Richmond Hill, Ontario L4B 2N5.

Library of Congress Cataloging-in-Publication Data
Gabler, Mirko.
    Brakus, Krakus... / by Mirko Gabler.
    Summary: When Mr. Skola takes the children in his
Travel Club to a mysterious Bohemian castle, the
resident ghost has some trouble with his spells and
turns the children into assorted animals.
    ISBN 0-8050-1963-4 (alk. paper)
    [1. Ghosts—Fiction. 2. Magic—Fiction. 3. School
field trips—Fiction.] I. Title.
PZ7.G1154Br 1993   [E]—dc20   92-25819

Printed in the United States of America
on acid-free paper. ∞

10 9 8 7 6 5 4 3 2 1

n a fine Sunday morning in May, Mr. Skola's Tourist Club
hit the road again. Every weekend the Club roamed the
countryside of Bohemia, looking for a new adventure. Mr. Skola,
the teacher in charge, was a seasoned traveler who, despite his
age, still had plenty of spark. And more than anything, he loved
to take the children to the kinds of places where parents would
never dare to go.

Today they set out for the mysterious castle of Kost.

The Club got off the train in a small village. Mr. Skola opened a map. But the map wasn't very helpful, because it was a map of the South China Sea, and that was not where they were going. Having traveled the world over, Mr. Skola had hundreds of maps at home, and it wasn't unusual for him to bring the wrong one.

"Look!" shouted someone. "It's over there!" Indeed, the mighty castle stood not far away, at the top of the hill. The children tied their shoelaces and raced up the road.

But Eva and Lenka, two very best friends, were in no hurry. They made crowns from dandelions and pretended to be princesses. Every now and then they whispered.

"What if it's haunted?" said Lenka.

"Most castles are!" Eva replied.

"Oooh…" They shivered. But only a little bit, because when the girls were together, they weren't afraid of anything.

Soon the Tourist Club reached the castle gate.

"Anybody home?" called Mr. Skola. "A tourist club is here to see the castle!"

A grumpy gatekeeper opened the door. "A tourist club, eh?" he sniffed. "Just make sure your tourists get out of here by five. There will be a full moon tonight, and I'm locking up early!"

"Haunted, is it?" asked Mr. Skola.

"See for yourself...." grumbled the gatekeeper, and handed Mr. Skola a tourist guide.

Mr. Skola led the way, and the children followed.

In the Great Hall, Mr. Skola opened the booklet.

"Aha!" he exclaimed. "There he is! Count Zuba the Great!" He pointed to a picture on the wall. "A master of astrology, geology, zoology, highway robbery, and the magic sciences..."

"And look at his ears!" someone shouted, when suddenly— *poof!*—Mr. Skola's hat was gone.

They found it in the kitchen, hanging on a chandelier.
"Hm...must be a window open somewhere..." said Mr. Skola,
and with a borrowed spear he set out to retrieve his hat. While he
fumbled with the heavy weapon, Eva and Lenka tiptoed into the
hallway to have a look around. As if drawn by some giant magnet,
the girls headed straight for the castle dungeon, where in a corner
stood a big black trunk.

It wasn't locked. As they peeked under the heavy lid, a silken glove slipped onto the floor. It was the kind that princesses wear to a ball. Lenka tried it on.

"It's just my size!" she said when suddenly, a voice came booming from above.

"Eva! Lenka! Where are you? It's time for lunch!" It was Mr. Skola. "Coming!" answered the girls. But then…they opened the trunk instead.

Meanwhile, up in the tower, Mr. Skola was finishing his plum cake. He yawned. "No climbing on the battlements!" he said and promptly fell asleep. While their teacher slept, the children explored the castle, and because they listened to his advice, no one came to any harm. When the clock struck five, it was time to go home. The Tourist Club crossed the drawbridge once again.

Bang! slammed the gate behind them, and the cranky gatekeeper turned the key.

Well rested, Mr. Skola beamed. "If we step on it, we'll be home in time for dinner!" The fresh air always gave him a good appetite, and he was already dreaming of the dumplings with gravy that Mrs. Skola would have waiting for him when he got home.

But that was not to be.

The train had barely left the station when Mr. Skola jumped out of his seat.

"Where is Eva?" he cried. "Where is Lenka?"

No one had seen them since lunchtime.

"Holy fiddlesticks!" Mr. Skola cried. "We must stop the train at once! It's an emergency! Emergency!"

And he pulled the emergency brake, and he pulled hard.

Suitcases flew and drinks spilled as the train shrieked to a halt.
"Eva and Lenka are locked up in the castle!" the children
explained as they scrambled out the door.

The sun was sinking fast, and they had no time to lose.
Breathless, they reached the castle gate. It was locked. They
pounded. They called.

"Eeevaaa! Lenkaaa!"

Suddenly the door opened and there stood two princesses.

"Good evening," they said. "You are just in time for the party!"

"A party?" blurted Mr. Skola. "What kind of party?"

"A birthday party!" whispered Eva. "The Count is three hundred years old today!" But Mr. Skola would have none of it.

"Absolutely not!" he cried. "We can't stay for any party! We haven't had dinner yet!"

Just then a pale gentleman appeared in the courtyard.

"Welcome, friends!" he said politely. "Come and join our little celebration!"

The children couldn't help staring at his ears.

"I…I…wish we c-c-could, sir," stammered Mr. Skola. "But we have school tomorrow, and the children have to go to bed early!"

"Oh, come now!" prodded the Count. "You must try the cake!"

Mr. Skola blinked.

"C-c-cake? A, er…w-w-what kind of cake?"

"Chocolate," said the Count. "With sprinkles!"

What was Mr. Skola to do? He followed the Count into the dining room. Lenka cut the cake with a sword and gave everyone a piece.

While they ate, the Count blew fireballs out of his ears and entertained the children with dangerous sword tricks. In their travels the children had seen a great many wonders, but never had they seen anyone swallow a real sword. Mr. Skola helped himself to a second slice.

"It's too bad he's a ghost," whispered Eva. "He could get a job in a circus!" The Count took a bow. Mr. Skola put down his plate. "Well, we'd better be off!" he said. "We've got a train to catch!"

"But you can't leave now!" protested the Count. "My best, my greatest, indeed my most dangerous trick is yet to come!"

Lenka gave Mr. Skola another slice, and the show continued. With a few words of magic, the Count turned himself into a handsome moose.

It was remarkable. Mr. Skola took a picture.

"What else can you turn into?" the children wanted to know.

"Name the beast and you shall have it!" bragged the Count. The children had a lot of ideas, and it was hard for them to make up their minds.

"Be a frog!" the children shouted. "Be a pig or a chicken! No, not a chicken! Be a zebra or an anteater!"

"Your wish is my command! An anteater it will be!" said the Count, and he began to chant this curious spell. "'Brakus, krakus, pidlibus, brakus, krakus, pidlibus...'"

Mr. Skola had just helped himself to his fourth
slice of cake, when suddenly—*poof!*

A powerful flash ripped through the castle,
and the dining room filled with smoke.
When the smoke cleared,
Mr. Skola gasped in horror.

The Tourist Club looked barely human. Some had feathers, some had fur, and some were scratching their fleas. Eva and Lenka, so elegant only a minute ago, had turned into a pair of scruffy crows. Mr. Skola was ready to faint. "They'll never let us on the train like this!" he wailed. "And what will the principal say?"

The Count's ears were now dangling to the floor.
    "Never fear, my friends!" he shouted. "I'll get it right! I'll look it
up in the library!" And he vanished into the darkness.

He returned with an enormous book. It was *The Great Book of Magic.* Snakeskins and dried insects spilled onto the table as he shuffled through the pages. But try as he might, Count Zuba the Great couldn't read a word of it.

"I must be going loony!" he moaned. "I must be getting old!"

"It's probably the moose head, sir," said Mr. Skola, trying to be helpful. He pulled up a chair, and for a long time the two of them puzzled over the book.

"Why, it's nothing but scribbles!" cried Mr. Skola at last.
Eva fluttered onto Mr. Skola's shoulder.
"The book is upside down!" she squawked. "It's upside down!"
"The book is what? Holy fiddlesticks!" exclaimed Mr. Skola.
He turned the book around and peered through his magnifying glass. The spell for Tourists in Trouble was right there in red ink under his very nose!

"'Brakus, krakus, pidlibus. Rah, rah, rah'!" Mr. Skola read. And—*crack!*—a wicked thunderbolt struck the roof and a terrific storm swept through the castle. Tails, snouts, ears, feathers, in fact all kinds of animal parts, flew out the window.

Mr. Skola looked at his watch. "The train!" he cried. "We'll miss the last train!"

The Tourist Club grabbed their backpacks and rushed out the door.

But where was the Count?

They found him in the courtyard, gazing at the moon. A white horse and a carriage stood ready by the gate.

"There's no need to rush," said the Count. "My carriage will take you home." The Count looked somehow…different.

"Your ears!" cried everyone. "Your piggy ears are gone!"

"Yes! Thanks to you my friends!" said Count Zuba the Great. To show his gratitude, he gave everyone a gold coin for a souvenir.

In fact, he was so pleased with his new ears that he let Eva and Lenka keep their fancy dresses and presented Mr. Skola with a big feather for his hat. The sleepy Tourist Club climbed into the carriage, and Mr. Skola locked the door.

"I hope you'll come to my castle again!" called the Count.

But the carriage was already flying through the air faster than any train could ever go.

The next morning the children were safely back in school. As usual, they entered the new adventure into their secret Travel Diary. They had almost finished, when Lenka said, "But what about those magic spells? We should write them down too!"

And so they did. With a red pencil, as Mr. Skola suggested.

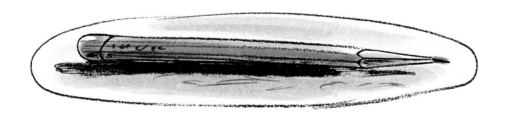

But their adventure didn't stay secret very long. Rumors of magic and gold soon spread through the school like wildfire, and everyone wanted to join the Club. Right away, the nosy principal asked to see the secret Diary. She didn't like what she saw.

"What? Flying in a carriage? What kind of a field trip is that? And what's this nonsense in red ink supposed to mean?" she puffed. "'Brakus, krakus'—what? 'Pidlibus'? Pidlibus indeed!"

And—*poof!*

But that, my friends, is another story.